To Savannah,

Always love your Abuela.

María de la Luz Reyes

How Will I TALK to ABUELA?

María de la Luz Reyes

Illustrations by
Blueberry Illustrations

IN MEMORIAM
Isabel G. Reyes
(March 5, 1908 – October 29, 1991)

Isabel G. Reyes, and María de la Luz Reyes, winter 1986.

Dedication:

This book is dedicated to
ALL
grandchildren and great-grandchildren
of
Isabel G. Reyes
who learned that
love needs no translation.

David's eyes scan every woman arriving from Los Angeles. He is excited to see his grandmother but nervous that she speaks mostly Spanish. David taps his fingernails on the wooden armrest. His legs dangle from his seat. He swings them back and forth, back and forth.

"Mom, will I be able to talk to Grandma?"
"Yes, David. You'll see how easy it will be when you meet her."
David has no trouble talking to anyone. But he isn't sure it will
be that easy with Grandma.

"Here she comes!" Mom cries out as she rushes to embrace Grandma. Grandma's short silvery hair glistens under the ceiling lights. Her skin is like caramel candy. Her dark eyes are the same color as Mom's eyes.

David stares at both women. For the very first time, he notices that Mom's skin is darker than his own. He is surprised to see that Grandma's smile is like Mom's big smile —"a smile that can fill a room," Dad always says.

Grandma greets David, "*Dah-VEED!*"
" '*Dah-veed*' is how David sounds in Spanish," Mom whispers.
"My name is *DAVID. DAVID HUBBARD*," I say, correcting
Grandma.

"*Dah-VEED Ah..bird*," Grandma repeats slowly. But, she skips the
H and makes the last part of my name sound like "bird"!

"In Spanish, the 'H' is silent," Mom explains.
"NO!... My name is *DAVID…DAVID HAA…HAA… HUBBARD*."
I repeat the "H" and exaggerate the sound for Grandma.

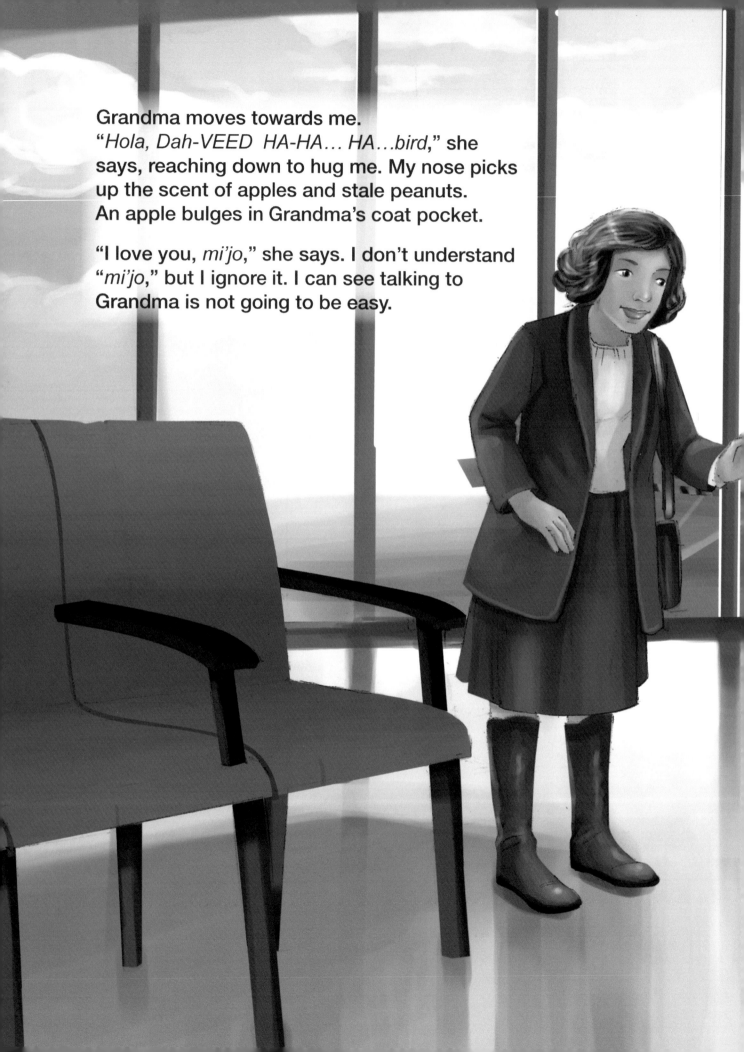

Grandma moves towards me.
"*Hola, Dah-VEED HA-HA… HA…bird*," she says, reaching down to hug me. My nose picks up the scent of apples and stale peanuts. An apple bulges in Grandma's coat pocket.

"I love you, *mi'jo*," she says. I don't understand "*mi'jo*," but I ignore it. I can see talking to Grandma is not going to be easy.

"I love you too, Grandma," I say, trying to make up for my little tantrum.

"*Abuela*," that's 'grandmother' in Spanish," Mom explains. "But you can call her '*abuelita*.' This shows respect and love," she adds. *Abuelita* takes my hand and we walk out to the car. My hand looks pasty against her tanned skin.

Later that afternoon, Mom says "*Mamá*, let's make some tortillas for dinner."
"*Sí, buena idea, mi'ja.*"
There's that word again! I'm not sure what it means, but again, I let it go.

I watch *Abuelita* and Mom pour flour into a big bowl. They mix water, salt and other ingredients. Pretty soon they have many small balls of dough. With a rolling pin, they roll each ball into something that looks like a big, thin cookie.

Abuelita puts the 'big cookie' on a *comal* to cook. I watch as *Abuelita* starts singing in Spanish. Mom hums along. Soon she joins in the singing, "*Ay, ay, ay, ay...*". They sing and laugh, as the stack of tortillas grows taller and taller. *Abuelita* and Mom chat mostly in Spanish. They are alone in their world.

I feel shut out. Mom has stopped translating for me.
"I DON'T UNDERSTAND!!...SPEAK ENGLISH!...PLEASE!"
I whine like a 3 year-old. They are too busy to hear me.
My eyes begin to sting. I hold back the tears for maybe 5
LONG minutes or more. Finally, *Abuelita* notices me.

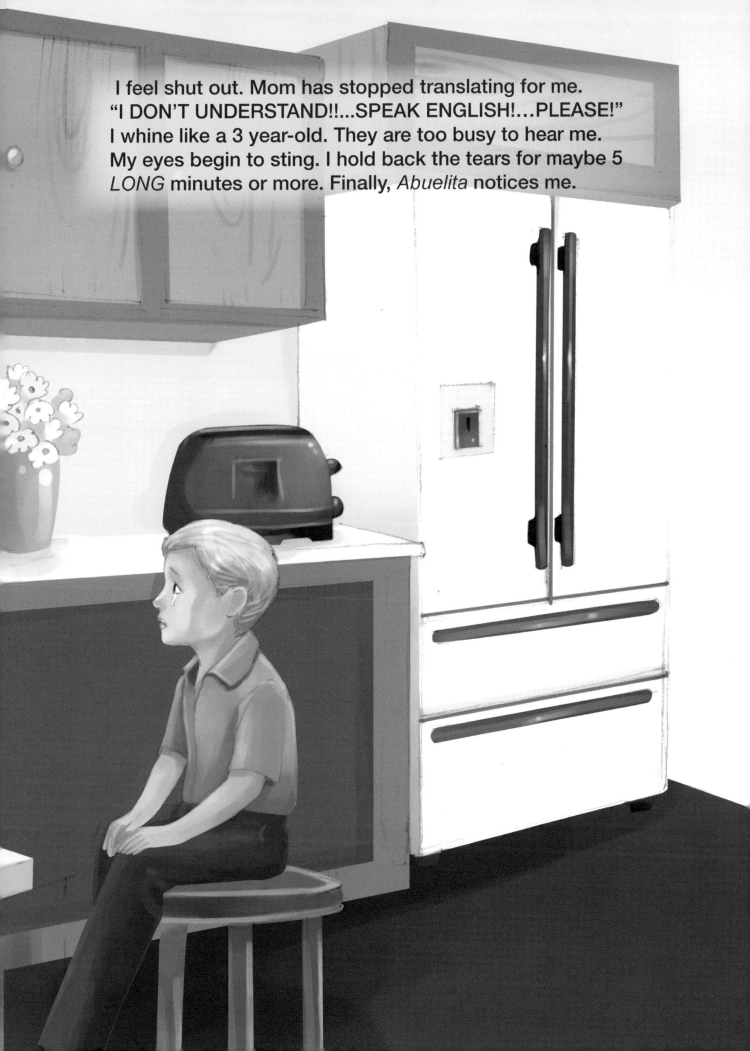

"*Oh, mi'jo, Abuelita is sorry*" she says in an English that sounds like Spanish. She puts her arms around me. Her hug is warm and sweet like Mom's.

Abuelita and Mom switch to English. *Abuelita* struggles, but she tries her best. I feel better. But, pretty soon, *Abuelita* starts sprinkling a Spanish word *here*, and a Spanish word *there*. I watch how she uses her hands to talk. I also watch her eyes, her mouth, and her face. These give me many clues that help me understand.

I watch Mom. She treats *every* Spanish word like a sweet, lost melody. It makes me happy.

When Dad gets home from work, he greets me with a hug. He kisses Mom and rushes to the kitchen to give *Abuelita* a hug.
"Hi, it's good to see you," he says to *Abuelita*.

"*Sí, mi'jo*," she says returning the hug.
There is that word again! Dad smiles when he hears it.
"How was your flight?" he asks.
Abuelita answers in her best English, but Dad is distracted by the smell of hot tortillas.
"Mmm…may I have one now?" he asks.

"*Sí, sí*." *Abuelita* invites Dad to take a tortilla. Dad grabs the top tortilla and hands me one. "Here's how you eat this, David. You spread a little butter on it, then you roll it like a cigar."

In a flash, the butter disappears on the warm tortillas. I try to roll my tortilla like Dad's and bite into it quickly before the butter drips on the kitchen floor. I have little success. Mom and *Abuelita* laugh.

After dinner *Abuelita* invites us to play *lotería*.
I am puzzled. Dad pulls up a chair and sits at the table.
"*Sí*. Let's play, David. *Lotería* is Mexican bingo," Mom explains.

I sit confused, but wait as *Abuelita* passes out a bingo-like card
to each of us. In place of numbers and letters, *lotería* cards
have pictures of people, plants, and other things in the squares.
There is also a deck of cards with each picture. *Abuelita*
explains the game. If our card has the picture of the
object she calls, we cover it. Four in a row makes bingo.

Suddenly, Mom blurts out "!ESPERA!
...WAIT, MAMÁ! I'll get pinto beans to
cover the squares."
"PINTO BEANS???" Dad and I cackle.
"That's the way we played lotería
when I was a little girl," Mom
explains. She gives each of
us a little pile of dry beans.

Our laughter bounces off the kitchen walls. I can't believe we are playing with pinto beans! I giggle.

"*¿Listos?*... Ready?"... *Abuelita* calls the first card from the stack.

"*El pino (peenoh),*" she says as she shows a pine tree.

"*PEE??*...NO!!" Dad repeats the word in his pretend Spanish. He pronounces the word with mischief in his voice.

Mom laughs. *Abuelita* laughs. I laugh.

"*Muy bien,*" *Abuelita* says. Then she waits for us to find the picture.

Abuelita **calls** *la mano*.
"*La MAH*?...NO!!" Dad clowns around.
We squeal with laughter. The small card shows a hand.
I find the picture on my card.

"*El sol*" is the next card. I find the picture of the sun on my card.
Pretty soon we are all repeating the Spanish words. This pleases
Abuelita. Dad keeps butchering the words. *Abuelita* still smiles.
I laugh so hard my stomach hurts. So many Spanish
words are spinning and twirling in my head!

"Your Spanish sounds like you're from Ohio!" Mom says.

When the game ends, *Abuelita* wraps me in her arms and says, "Good night, *Dah-VEED HA-HA..HA..bird*. I love you, mi'jo."

I smile. *This time* I don't correct how *Abuelita* says my name.

"I love you, too, Aboo-lee-tah." *Abuelita* doesn't correct my Spanish.

"I had so much fun today. Thank you," I tell her.

She smiles and kisses me. I skip to my bedroom.

Mom enters my bedroom. She sits on the edge of my bed.
"Mom, are you Mexican?" I ask.

"I was born in Texas, but my family's background is Mexican.
So, I am American AND Mexican."

"Hmm…and… Dad, what is he?"

"His great-grandparents came from Germany so he is part
German and American," Mom explains.

"So,…am *I Mexican*?"

"You are American with Mexican and German background."

"Is that good, Mom?"

"Not good…WONDERFUl!" she says planting a kiss on my cheek.

"But, it's time for bed! Good night, David. Sweet dreams."

"Not David. *Dah-VEED! Dah-VEED Ha-Ha…Ha..bird*,"

I grin as Mom turns off the light.

GLOSSARY

abuela	grandmother
abuelita	an affectionate term for grandmother
buena idea	good idea
comal	cast iron griddle used for making tortillas
espera	wait
hola	hello
lotería	literal meaning is 'lottery"; a traditional Mexican game similar to bingo except it uses pictures instead of numbers and letters
mano	hand
mi'jo/mi'ja	an affectionate and short version of "mi hijo," my son, or "mi hija", my daughter
muy bien	very good, very well
pino	pine tree
sí	yes
sol	sun
tortilla	a type of flat, round bread made with flour, a staple of Mexican food

The End